This book belongs to

and

....

For my fabulous nieces Eva and Anna, experts at hide and seek xx—K.M^cK.
To my woollie consultants Harry, Ellie and Meggie—J.S.

OXFORD
UNIVERSITY PRESS

Great Clarendon Street, Oxford OX2 6DP

Oxford University Press is a department of the University of Oxford.
It furthers the University's objective of excellence in research, scholarship,
and education by publishing worldwide.

Oxford is a registered trade mark of Oxford University Press in the UK and in
certain other countries

Text © Oxford University Press 2018
Illustrations © Jon Stuart 2018

The moral rights of the author/illustrator have been asserted Database right
Oxford University Press (maker)

First published in 2018

British Library Cataloguing in Publication Data
Data available

ISBN: 978-0-19-274785-3 (paperback)

10 9 8 7 6 5 4 3 2 1

Printed in China

Paper used in the production of this book is a natural, recyclableproduct made
from wood grown in sustainable forests.The manufacturing process conforms to
the environmental regulations of the country of origin.

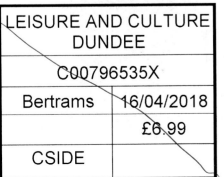

'My name's Zip.
Today I'm feeling
playful!'

'I'm Baby Woolly.
I'm the smallest
Woolly!'

'Hello, I'm Bling.
Do you like my
stripy tights?'

'I'm Puzzle.
I'm good
at sorting
things out!'

THE WOOLLIES

Flying High

Kelly McKain
Jon Stuart

OXFORD
UNIVERSITY PRESS

The Woollies were snoozing
by their house.

Suddenly there was a
pptttappttpptt noise.
It woke Baby Woolly up.

The noise gave Baby
Woolly an idea.

'Imagi-knit!' he said.

'I made a plane!' cried Baby Woolly.
'Look, Zip! Look at me fly!'

Baby Woolly looped the loop
and zigged and zagged.
He even flew upside down!

But then . . . oh no! The control got stuck, Baby Woolly could not stop. 'Help! Help! Help!' he yelped.

'My woolly friends will never find me now!' he wailed.
'And I'm stuck! I'll have to stay here forever! ALL ON MY OWN!'

Suddenly something moved in the bush.
'Argh!' cried Baby Woolly. 'A wild thing
is coming to eat me!'

The wild thing was only a noisy crow.
'CAW! CAW! CAW!' it went, and then it flew away.
'I know how I can get rescued,' said Baby Woolly.
'I need to make some noise, like that crow! Imagi-knit!'

"Help! Over here!"

"Help! Over here!"

"Help! Over here!"

"Help! Over here!"

Puzzle, Bling, and Zip heard the noise.
'Over there!' cried Bling, and off they zoomed.

But Puzzle went so fast,

the helicopter began to wobble . . .

. . . and tipped Bling and Zip out!

'Oh no!' they cried. 'Imagi-knit!'

'You found me!' said Baby Woolly,
as Zip untangled him.

'We heard your big booming voice
coming from your clever machine,'
said Zip.

The Woollies climbed up
into the helicopter.

And they zoomed home together.

'I'm tired now!' yawned Baby Woolly.
'Nap time for baby flyers.'

And soon Baby Woolly was dreaming
of a whole new woolly adventure.

ZZZ
ZZZZ

A note for grown-ups

Oxford Owl is a FREE and easy-to-use website packed with support and advice about everything to do with reading.

Informative videos

Hints, tips and fun activities

Top tips from top writers for reading with your child

Help with choosing picture books

For this expert advice and much, much more about how children learn to read and how to keep them reading ...

LOOK
for Oxford Owl
www.oxfordowl.co.uk